CUMBRIA LIBRARIES

D1589013

T!
L
w
lil

ORCHARD BOOKS
Carmelite House
50 Victoria Embankment
London EC4Y 0DZ

First published as BUMBLEBEE VERSUS SCUZZARD in 2015 in the
United States by Little, Brown and Company

This edition published by Orchard Books in 2016

HASBRO and its logo, TRANSFORMERS, TRANSFORMERS
ROBOTS IN DISGUISE, the logo and all related characters are
trademarks of Hasbro and are used with permission.

© 2016 Hasbro. All Rights Reserved.

A CIP catalogue record for this book is available
from the British Library.

ISBN 978 1 40834 490 3

1 3 5 7 9 10 8 6 4 2

Printed and bound by CPI Group (UK) Ltd, Croydon, CR0 4YY

Orchard Books
An imprint of Hachette Children's Group
Part of The Watts Publishing Group Limited
An Hachette UK Company
www.hachette.co.uk

MIX
Paper from
responsible sources
FSC® C104740

The paper and board used in this book are made from wood from
responsible sources.

ROBOTS
TO THE RESCUE

BY JOHN SAZAKLIS

ORCHARD

MEET THE TEAM:

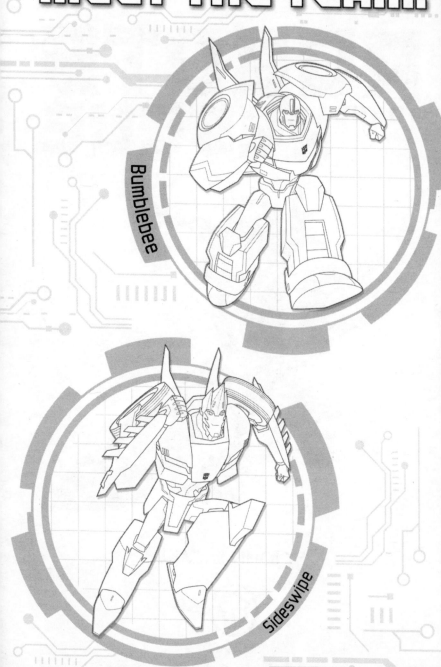

Bumblebee

Sideswipe

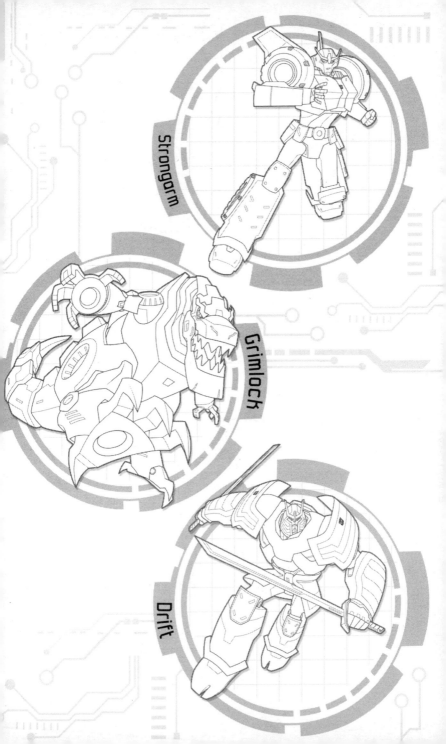

Strongarm

Grimlock

Drift

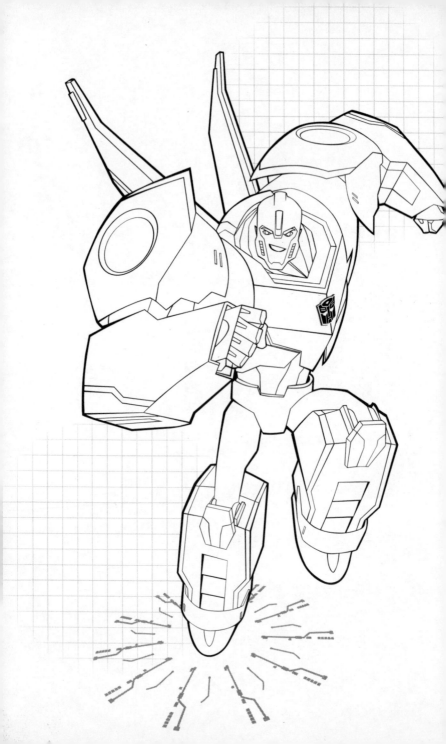

CONTENTS

FLICK TO SCROLL

STATUS REPORT: A prison ship from the planet Cybertron has crashed on Earth, and deadly robot criminals – the Decepticons – have escaped.

It's up to a team of Autobots to find them and get them back into stasis. Lieutenant Bumblebee, rebellious Sideswipe and police trainee, Strongarm, have taken the Groundbridge from Cybertron to Earth to track them down.

Along with bounty hunter, Drift, reformed Decepticon, Grimlock, and the malfunctioning pilot of the ship, Fixit, as well as the two humans who own the scrapyard where the ship crashed, Russell Clay and his dad, Denny, the Robots in Disguise must find the Decepticons, before they destroy the entire world …

CHAPTER ONE

"STOP IN YOUR TRACKS, Decepticon!" shouted Bumblebee. "You're under arrest!"

The Autobot leader blasted his plasma cannon. The moving target leapt from side to side then somersaulted over the Cybertronian lieutenant, landing behind him. Then he shoved Bumblebee to the ground.

"Is that the best you got, law-bot?" he taunted.

"Training's over!" Bumblebee said. The Decpticon was really his team-mate, the young, energetic and rebellious Autobot called Sideswipe.

"You're scrap metal!" Sideswipe yelled.

"Enough!" Bumblebee said, with a laugh.

Sideswipe smiled, extended his arm, and helped his sparring partner up off the ground.

"Pretty impressive," Bumblebee said. "You've got some nice moves, but the tough-bot attitude might be a bit over the top, don't you think?"

The young Autobot laughed. "But you've got to be a tough-bot if you want to intimidate those Decepticons, Bee."

"Thanks for the advice," Bumblebee replied. "Now, who's next?"

The Autobot leader scanned the scrapyard that currently served as their team headquarters and training area.

Located on the outskirts of Crown City on planet Earth, the scrapyard belonged to a pair of humans: Denny Clay and his son, Russell. The Clays had befriended Bumblebee and his robot team when they'd arrived on Earth on their mission – to track down and capture the escaped Decepticon criminals from the planet Cybertron.

"It is my turn, sir," called out Strongarm. The young police trainee dutifully walked over to the centre of the training area.

Back on Cybertron, Strongarm had been a member of the police force serving under Lieutenant Bumblebee. Now she helped to serve and protect anyone or anything that could come to harm at the hands of the Autobots' evil enemies on Earth – the Decepticons.

"Let's see if your moves are as good as mine," Sideswipe said to her. "Not everyone gets the best of Bee. But I did!"

"Show some respect, Sideswipe," replied Strongarm. "You may have 'street smarts' back home, but you're no intellitron. Bumblebee is your commanding officer, you should treat him with respect!"

"You're right," Sideswipe snapped back. "So I have to listen to *him*. Not *you*!"

"Fine," huffed the police-bot. "Who says I want to waste nanocycles talking to you, anyway?" Strongarm smiled. "I'd have to use smaller words and talk … very … slowly."

"Enough!" Bumblebee said, exasperated. "We are all on the same team, whether we like to admit it or not. The real foes are out there and we need to be prepared. Something terrible is on the horizon and, by the AllSpark, I sure hope we can handle it!"

"Yes, sir," Strongarm said. "Let's continue training."

"Where are Grimlock and Drift?" Sideswipe asked.

Grimlock was a dinobot and a former Decepticon, but he had joined the Autobots, and Drift was a bounty hunter. They were both part of Bumblebee's ragtag team.

"Drift has been excused from today's training," Bumblebee replied. "He took a Groundbridge to an area with an allegedly high concentration of Energon. You know how he likes his solo missions."

"Yeah, Drift sure is a real-deal tough-bot," Sideswipe said. "I'm glad he's on our side."

Bumblebee chuckled. "I asked him to check it out and report back to me," the leader said.

"If there *is* Energon out there, we'll travel to the location and harvest the power source right away."

"Excellent." Strongarm cheered. "Another mission!"

"I totally understand your enthusiasm, Strongarm," Bumblebee replied. "Things have been a little quiet around here."

"Yeah, quiet until the storm hits," Sideswipe said, slamming his fist into his palm. "I'm ready for whatever the Decepticons have got!"

"I have a feeling the Decepticons will be causing their usual destruction before too long," Bumblebee replied.

The others nodded grimly.

Strongarm tried to lighten the mood. "Speaking of destruction, what's

Grimlock up to today?"

"He's recharging on top of a pile of old cars," a voice answered.

The Autobots turned to see Russell, their twelve-year-old human friend. "Grimlock found a nice sunny spot, and he's lying in it like a big lizard."

"Hey, Russell," Bumblebee said. "What's up?"

"Shouldn't you be at lob-ball practice?" asked Sideswipe.

Russell chuckled. "Here on Earth, it's called rugby."

"Oh, right," Sideswipe said, trying to remember the word. "Rug-by."

"And there's no practice today. It's the Easter break," Russell continued.

"A break?" Strongarm asked, puzzled.

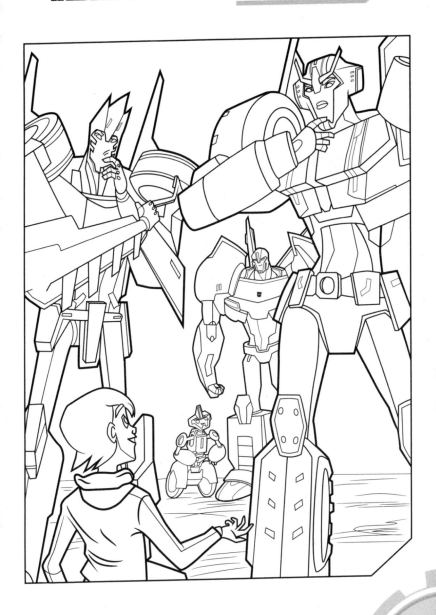

Suddenly, Fixit rolled into the training area from behind a dented billboard.

"Who's had a break?" Fixit asked. "It's about time! I've been itching to repaint … repaste … repair something."

Fixit the mini-con had been the pilot of the prison transport ship *Alchemor* – the same ship that had crashed to Earth and let loose the Decepticon criminals. Now he was part of Team Bee as the resident handy-bot.

After the ship's crash, Fixit had developed a minor stutter, but he normally managed to correct his vocabulary with a quick check.

The mini-con weaved in and out between the legs of the Autobots, twitching his digits excitedly.

"No one had anything break," Bumblebee said, looking himself over. "As far as I can tell."

Russell laughed. "A break is another way of saying we're taking a holiday from school."

"What's a holiday?" Strongarm asked.

"It's time off," Sideswipe replied.

Strongarm's optic sensors opened wide with surprise. "Who would want to take time off from school?"

"Not Miss Perfect Attendance, I'm sure," Sideswipe retorted.

"Every single cycle!" Strongarm announced proudly.

"Really? I'm very impressed, trainee," Bumblebee said to her. "That's an excellent record!"

"I know!" Strongarm beamed.

Sideswipe rolled his optic sensors.

"Anyway," Russell interrupted. "My friends Sam and Mo are going away with their families for the next week and, well, I'm kind of stuck here, where nothing exciting has happened in ages." The boy kicked a stone and sat on an overturned shopping trolley.

"That's not so bad," Fixit replied. "I'm stumped … stunned … stuck here all the time when all the other bots are out on missions or when they play games together."

"Every team member's duty is very important," Bumblebee explained. "Especially yours, Fixit."

Sideswipe sighed. "All right. There's

only so much sappy goodness this bot
can take before he gets brain rust."

He walked over and crouched near the
mini-con.

"So, you wanna play lob-ball with us?
You got it!"

He gave a loud whistle and there was
a loud smashing sound from across
the scrapyard. Grimlock was
awake.

"Big G!" Sideswipe yelled. "We're playing lob-ball with Fixit. Go long!

"Finally!" Grimlock exclaimed, as he stretched his limbs. "Something to do that involves some action!"

Fixit rubbed his digits together with anticipation and excitement.

"Excellent. What's my position?"

Sideswipe smirked and picked up the mini-con.

"Ball," he said.

Then, in one deft movement, he hurled Fixit through the air, straight at Grimlock.

"*AAAAAAAAAH!*" the mini-con screeched as he became a tiny dot against the sky.

Bumblebee sighed and shook his head.

"When I said we need to focus on working as a team, this is not what I had in mind."

CHAPTER TWO

GRIMLOCK JUMPED OFF THE PILE OF cars and dashed into action. Shifting into his bot mode, he grabbed an old metal bathtub and scrunched it onto his head.

With his makeshift helmet secured, the dinobot rushed toward Fixit, all the while giving a running commentary.

"This is it, ladies and gentlebots! Only mere nanocycles left in the game. Cybertron lob-ball legend 'Gridlock' Grimlock sprints to catch the final pass. Will it be the winning play? Keep your optics open. You won't want to miss a single thing!"

"Gridlock Grimlock! Gridlock Grimlock!" chanted Sideswipe.

Grimlock caught Fixit, pulled him into his chest, turned and charged in the opposite direction. When he reached the end of the scrapyard, he hoisted Fixit high into the air.

"Gridlock Grimlock wins the game for Team Bee!" he roared. "And the crowd goes wild!"

Sideswipe turned on his car radio speakers and blasted some loud music.

"Go, Grimlock, it's your *bot*day!" he sang, dancing to the beat.

Caught up in the excitement, Grimlock went to throw Fixit onto the ground as if he were a real ball.

"Grimlock, no!" Strongarm shouted.

Quick as a flash, she and Bumblebee shifted into their vehicle modes and

ROBOTS TO THE RESCUE

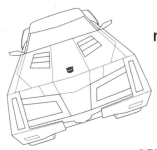

rushed to the rescue.

They got to Grimlock just as he threw the mini-con. Bumblebee's car tyres screeched and squealed and kicked up dirt as he turned at high speed. The yellow car opened his trunk, and Fixit landed safely inside.

Bumblebee then changed back into bot mode, with the mini-con in his arms.

Fixit's gears rattled dizzily. "I think that's enough feet … feed … fieldwork for one day. Thanks."

As Bumblebee readied himself to tell Grimlock off, Sideswipe snatched Fixit from his arms.

"FOUL!" shouted Sideswipe, sprinting to the other end of the yard.

Grimlock bounded after him.

Bumblebee threw up his hands in frustration and looked at the sky. When he felt troubled, he sought guidance from his hero, Optimus Prime.

"Optimus, if you can hear me, please give me a sign. Anything that will— Aha!"

A shiny object glinted in the sunlight, catching Bumblebee's attention.

For a moment, the Autobot saw the reflection of Optimus Prime, but it was gone as soon as it appeared.

The same object gave Bumblebee an idea. Shifting into vehicle mode, he sped past the other Autobots and reached the end of the scrapyard first. He switched back and climbed inside a truck with the shiny object attached – a huge magnet.

Bumblebee pulled down on a large lever and the machine whirred to life. The magnet dropped towards the ground – at the same exact moment that Grimlock and Sideswipe raced by underneath!

CLANG!

CLANG!

The robots were yanked off their feet and right onto the magnet.

"*AAH!*" they shouted.

As he flailed around, Sideswipe dropped Fixit, but luckily Strongarm was there to catch him.

The mini-con's optic sensors were swirling wildly.

"Strongarm, how long have you had a sitter ... a sitar ... a sister?" he asked as he saw double. "Are you twigs ... twits

... twins? She looks just like you! It's a pleasure to meet you, my dear!"

"Hey, what's the big idea?" Sideswipe yelled, as he dangled from the magnet.

"Game over," Bumblebee said sternly. "You have to be nice to Fixit. We're all on the same team."

"Sorry, Fixit," Sideswipe said.

Grimlock looked down and saw his feet hanging high above the yard.

"I can fly!" he cheered.

Bumblebee pulled the lever again, deactivating the magnet, and released the two enormous Autobots onto the ground below.

CRASH!

Suddenly, Denny Clay came running into the scrapyard. He was flustered and gasping for breath.

"Dad, is everything OK?" Russell asked.

"You'll never guess what happened!" Denny blurted out.

"What is it?"

"It's something that's going to change our lives for ever!"

Russell looked at the robots. "What could possibly change our lives more than our new houseguests?"

"It's not kittens, is it?" Grimlock asked warily. The dinobot had a strange fear of cats. "I think I hear Drift calling me. I'll go and see what he wants." The dinobot ran away to the other side of the scrapyard, much to the bewilderment of his team-mates.

Denny sat down to catch his breath. He was huffing and puffing and wheezing.

Fixit rolled over and scanned him. "I'm not familiar with organic biology, but it appears that Denny Clay is running on fumes. Does he need more fuel? I have my grandbot's home remedy right here in the holo-scroll!" Fixit rolled away into the command centre.

After what felt like an eternity for the anxious group, Denny finally caught his breath and said, "An old friend of mine called to say he's got two amazing items for sale. You'll never guess! OK, I'll tell you. Vintage pinball machines!"

Russell slumped his shoulders disappointedly. "Oh. More junk for the junkyard."

"Hey, these things are super rare!" Denny said excitedly. "They're not exactly in working order, but it'll give us something to do together when we repair them."

"Pardon us for asking," Bumblebee interrupted Denny, "but what are pinball machines? Are they good or bad?"

"Do they shoot pins?" Strongarm asked curiously.

"Ha, no!" Denny said, with a laugh. "They're old-fashioned coin-operated arcade games."

"Oooh, games!" Sideswipe said.

"Don't get too excited," Russell responded. "They're ancient history. Just like everything else in this place."

Denny tried to cheer up his son. "Come on, Rusty. We'll take a little road trip together. It'll be a blast and a half! Things seem to be quiet here."

"Your father is right," Bumblebee said. "I'm confident we can manage for a while without you. Go and enjoy yourselves."

"Fine," Russell said. Then he whispered to Sideswipe: "Call us immediately if

something exciting
happens, so I don't
die of boredom."

"You got it, dude,"
Sideswipe whispered back.

As Denny and Russell
headed inside to prepare for
their trip, the Autobots dispersed
throughout the yard.

Grimlock returned with a brave face.
"Hey, I don't think that was Drift calling
me after all!" he said with a chuckle.

Seeing that he was alone, a wave of
panic gripped the dinobot.

"Oh, no!" He gulped. "Where have
the others gone? Maybe the kittens have
got them!"

CHAPTER THREE

"ALL ABOARD!" DENNY SAID, AS HE climbed into his pick-up truck.

Russell climbed into the passenger seat and buckled himself in.

His father was elated. "I can't wait to get my hands on those fantastic fixer-uppers!"

"So, where are we headed exactly?" Russell asked.

"My old school friend, Doug Castillo, owns an arcade near the amusement park," Denny said. "It's called Doug's Den. He's got all kinds of cool old-school video games. I always wanted to take you there when you were younger, but I never got the chance."

As Denny lost himself in thinking about the past, Russell fell silent and stared out of the window. His father hadn't been around much when he was growing up. But now, with his mum working abroad, Russell was spending a lot more time with his dad.

It wasn't long after Russell moved to the scrapyard, or, as his father called it, the "vintage salvage depot for the discriminating nostalgist," that the Autobots had literally crash-landed into their lives.

Russell watched the trees whizz by and wondered how vast the universe must be if alien robots really existed on other planets. Especially when those robots were sentient beings with the ability to transform their bodies into the shape of vehicles or animals while battling one another right outside his very home.

The pick-up continued over the bridge leading into the city. Denny rolled down the window and turned on the radio, sighing happily. "It's good to get away!"

Meanwhile, underneath the bridge in a murky marsh, a large metallic object glinted in the sun. Part of it was submerged in water and most of the exterior was damaged.

When the Alchemor crashed to Earth, a number of prison cells known as stasis pods had been scattered across the surrounding area. Those pods contained Cybertron's most violent criminals – Decepticons.

Unfortunately, some of them had escaped their pods, and it was the Autobots' mission to round them up.

Now, this particular pod started to shift and rattle as the prisoner stirred within.

CRACK.

CRACK.

CRACK.

A sharp, pointed beak was pecking its way out, like a bird hatching from an egg. Finally, it broke free from the stasis pod.

SKRAaaaCK!

An oversized, rust-coloured, vulturish

Decepticon emerged. Stretching his long neck and long wings, the creature stepped, blinking, into the sun. It scoured the terrain for food.

"I HUNGER!" he screeched.

His raspy, grainy voice startled a nearby frog, which leapt into the water.

Following the movement, the Decepticon stabbed at the water with his beak – and pulled out a soggy boot.

"Meh!" he exclaimed in disgust and flung it aside. "Where am I?" He turned his head from side to side. "This is not Cybertron. We must have landed on another, far inferior, planet."

Then he spotted a discarded tin can. "Is that the best sustenance this ragged rock has to offer?" he squawked. He pinched the can with his beak and swallowed it in one gulp.

Suddenly, the Decepticon felt a wonderful sensation. His body rippled with energy – and grew bigger and more menacing. "Hmm," he said, with a horrible grin. "This rock may have something to offer me after all!"

Russell and his father finally arrived at the amusement park and drove around to where Doug's Den was located.

A man with glasses and a ponytail was waiting for them, a big grin on his face. Russell guessed that it was Doug.

"Denny, you ol' sea dog!" Doug yelled as Russell and his dad exited the truck. He squeezed Denny in a bear hug that lifted him off the ground.

"Dougie, you haven't changed a bit. I want you to meet my son, Rusty."

"It's Russell, actually," Russell said.

"And I'm Doug," the man said, with a wink. "Come on in, I'll show you around!"

Russell and his father walked through the arcade, looking at all the games.

There was one where a yellow circle with a mouth ate white dots while running from ghosts. Another one starred a short plumber with a moustache that had to save a princess.

"Wow! This is awesome!" Denny gushed. "What do you think, Rusty?"

"I think it's cool … but a little old."

"Russell, apologise!" his father scolded.

Doug laughed. "No offence taken. The boy's right. Kids today have portable, digital, highly advanced technology in the palm of their hands. Why waste their time with these clunky old dinosaurs?"

"You don't need to tell me about clunky dinosaurs," Denny said. He looked at Russell with a gleam in his eye. Russell smiled knowingly.

"I might as well turn this place into a museum," Doug continued. "I'll charge people to come in and hear me say, 'The first coin-operated pinball machine was introduced in 1931.'"

Denny brightened. "And speaking of pinball machines … "

"Oh, yes! Right this way."

The group circled around back to the loading dock, where two old pinball machines stood wrapped in plastic.

Russell could see the detailed illustrations painted on the back of each game. They were of an adventurer wearing a leather jacket and brown hat. In one, he was swinging on a rope over a pit of cobras surrounded by flames.

Hmm, maybe these things aren't so

boring after all, Russell thought.

About half an hour later, they were back on the road again.

"I can't wait to tinker with them," Denny said. "Maybe even put some of the Autobot technology in 'em!"

Rusty smiled. The trip had turned out to be a fun adventure after all.

But when they reached the bridge, Denny slammed on the brakes.

There appeared to be a traffic jam, with several bystanders looking over the side of the bridge.

Suddenly, a screeching creature swooped up into the air.

"Is that a hawk?" Russell asked.

"It looks more like a vulture," Denny said, puzzled.

Just as suddenly, it dived towards them.
Denny and Russell saw the Decepticon
logo on the vulture's metallic hide.

"I wish we had some Autobot tech
with us right now!" Russell yelled. "It's
a Decepticon!"

49

CHAPTER FOUR

SCREEEEEECH!

The sound of metal scraping metal was ear-piercing as the Decepticon dug his claws into the bonnet of the truck.

"A Decepticon prisoner must have escaped from a stasis pod!" Russell cried.

"Rusty, look out!" shouted Denny.

The vulture pecked at the windscreen glass with his giant beak. Thin cracks crept across it in a spiderweb pattern.

"We've got to get Bumblebee and the others!" Russell yelled.

"But first, we gotta get this thing away from the people," replied Denny. He wrenched the wheel, making the truck veer off the road and head to the woods.

The Decepticon hissed in surprise and dug his talons in deeper to maintain a grip on the car bonnet.

"We're taking the scenic route, you big buzzard," Denny said.

Rusty fumbled for the radio on the truck's dashboard. But the truck's tyres bumped along the uneven terrain, jostling Russell. He accidentally dropped the radio, and it slid under his seat.

Denny shouted a warning as the Decepticon reared his head back for another attack. "Get down and cover your head!"

The vulture stabbed at the glass again, breaking it with his beak.

SHUNK!

"AAAAAAAAH!" Denny yelled and

accidentally turned on the windscreen wipers. They began swishing from side to side, momentarily hypnotising the rampaging robot.

Screeching with annoyance, the Decepticon chomped down and ripped them off. He chewed them but found them unsatisfactory.

"BLEH!" he screeched, spitting them out. Then he turned to attack again. The windscreen wouldn't take another hit.

Denny used his wits and, in a last-ditch effort, squirted the bad birdbot with windscreen-wiper fluid.

SQUIRRRT!

The liquid coated the vulture's face, blinding him. Flailing his wings, he lost balance and lurched backwards.

Denny spun the wheel one more time, causing the truck to swerve in a complete circle. The Decepticon tumbled off the car bonnet, clawed at the air and slammed into a nearby tree trunk.

BAM!

Unfortunately, one of the pinball machines was also jarred loose and fell off the back of the truck, onto the ground. The glass display shattered into a million pieces. The metal gears and ball bearings rolled over the grass, glinting and shimmering under the sun.

This caught the vulture's attention, and he descended on the arcade game, ripping it apart. The priceless pinball machine was now nothing more than a worthless chew toy.

"Oh, man!" Denny lamented, looking over his shoulder.

Without a moment to lose, he slammed his foot on the accelerator and the pick-up truck sped off towards the scrapyard.

Russell finally got his hands on the radio and tried to contact the Autobots.

"There's no answer, Dad," he said.

Denny gulped and tried not to look worried. He wiped the sweat off his brow with the back of his hand.

"Do you think our friends are in trouble?" Russell asked.

"Only one way to find out," replied Denny. "We're almost there."

CHAPTER FIVE

WHEN RUSSELL AND DENNY
arrived, they jumped out of the truck and
rushed into the scrapyard, only to find it
eerily quiet.

"Where is everyone?" Russell asked.

"I hope they're OK," Denny said.

With his father, the young boy ran up
and down the aisles of piled junk, calling
out the names of their robot friends.

Suddenly, there was a loud crash and
crunching of metal, followed by painful
grunts and the sound of a struggle.

"Oh, no!" Russell exclaimed. "That
sounds like trouble to me!"

The humans sprinted through the
maze-like scrapyard until they discovered

the source of the commotion.

There, in a clearing between the rusty lawnmowers and a broken tractor, was an Autobot pile-up!

Sideswipe was sprawled on the bottom. Lying on top of him was Bumblebee, then Strongarm, and finally Grimlock.

They all looked exhausted and defeated. Russell noticed that the robots were barely moving.

"Our friends picked the wrong time to be playing games," Denny said. "Now what are we going to do?"

Rusty cupped his hands around his mouth and shouted. "HELP!"

The Autobots turned towards the worried humans.

"Welcome back!" Sideswipe said cheerily from the bottom of the pile.

The robots climbed off one another and helped Sideswipe to his feet. Clutched close to his chest was a large concrete wrecking ball.

"We finally played a proper game of lob-ball," he said, happily. "And this ball is much better than Fixit!"

"I agree," said the mini-con, scurrying out from behind a rubbish bin.

"See?" Sideswipe said. "Now I can finally do *THIS*!"

With one swift motion, he smashed the wrecking ball into the ground, making a cloud of dust and debris.

Bumblebee walked over and asked, "How was your trip?"

"Terrible!" Russell exclaimed. "While you guys were running around, we were running for our lives!"

"What happened?" Strongarm asked, suddenly serious.

"We were attacked by a flying Decepticon," Denny told the group.

Stunned, the Autobots looked at one another. Without a moment to lose, they shifted into their vehicle modes.

Bumblebee quickly became a sleek yellow sports car and scooped up Denny into his driving seat.

Sideswipe transformed into his flashier red sports car and took Russell.

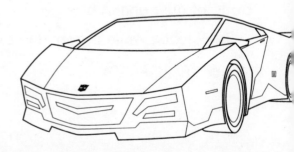

Strongarm took her police-car form.

Fixit and Grimlock followed along in their bot modes because they didn't have vehicle appearances to change into.

Together, they all zoomed back to the command centre they'd set up at the end of the junkyard.

Once they were outside the command centre, the Autobots changed back into bot mode and entered. Fixit rolled to the control panel and checked the map on the big computer screen. There was a blinking dot near their location.

"It would appear that there is another Decepticon on the loon ... loop ... loose," he said.

"I told you we'd seen one," Denny replied. "It was like a bird."

"It had razor-sharp claws and a beak and wings!" Rusty added. "He almost made a meal out of the pick-up!"

Fixit clacked away on the keyboard, calling up all the flying Decepticons that had been on the *Alchemor*. A few seconds later, several images appeared on the holo-scroll.

Rusty and Denny pointed at their assailant simultaneously.

"That one!" they shouted.

"His name is Scuzzard," Bumblebee read. "And he's a Scavengebot. His abilities are similar to those of a Chompozoid."

"That's no good," Strongarm added.

"When those Decepticons consume metal, it super-charges their bodies until they become unstoppable."

"Scavengebots have the compulsion to tear everything apart before they consume it." Bumblebee explained. "Most of them are pretty harmless and feast on scrap metal. Not Scuzzard, though."

"Hmm, I seem to remember why he was imprisoned," Strongarm said. "He was arrested for laying waste to a good part of Kaon's industrial area. It took an entire squadron of the capital's police force to detain and contain him!"

Denny spoke up. "I can believe it! That thing is strong. We only just got away. It made a meal out of one of my poor pinball machines, too."

"So what's the plan, sir?" Strongarm asked Bumblebee.

"Good question," Bumblebee replied. "We need to lure him away from civilians, get him into a secluded area, and subdue him as quickly as possible."

"Finally!" Sideswipe said. "Just what

I needed to flex my pistons!"

Bumblebee smiled. "You've given me an idea, Sideswipe. We can send you out first … as a decoy."

"Wait, what?" replied the young Autobot. "That is a very bad idea."

"Not really," added Strongarm. "You're red, shiny and quick to catch attention. Perfect bait!"

"And you're fast," concluded Bumblebee.

Sideswipe tried to protest, but he couldn't help but agree with everything his team-mates said.

"You're right," he said, shaking his head. "I admit it – I make Decepticon hunting look good!" The hotshot Autobot

started admiring his own reflection in a
nearby mirror.

Strongarm aimed her blaster and
pulverised the mirror.

"Eek!" Grimlock shrieked. "That's
seven cycles of bad luck!"

"Get over yourself," Strongarm said to
Sideswipe.

"You get over *your*self!" Sideswipe
retorted.

"Let's get this mission over with,
please," Bumblebee interrupted. Then he
started to give orders to the rest of the
team. "Fixit, send us Scuzzard's
coordinates."

As the mini-con complied, Russell and
Denny consulted the map.

"Hmm, that buzzardbot seems to have

flown into town and is circling the area above my buddy's arcade," Denny observed.

"You have to move fast before he attacks!" Russell said.

"There's a mile of deserted road in the forest leading back here," Denny told Bumblebee. "It's a longer route, but you can avoid the bridge and being seen by humans."

"Thank you," Bumblebee said. Then he turned to Sideswipe.

"You will get Scuzzard's attention and lure him back to the deserted road. Strongarm and I will be waiting to form a triangulation and trap him with our neo-forges."

"What about me?" asked Grimlock.

"You will stay here. These Decepticons are unpredictable. If any more of them appear, we will need you as one of our last defenses here at the base."

"Oh, man!" Grimlock hung his head.

"OK, team," Bumblebee said. "Let's cruise down to bruise town!"

The Autobots stood still and stared at their leader. He kept trying to find a catchphrase, but had been less than successful.

Sideswipe smiled. "How 'bout we just rock and roll?"

Bumblebee sighed. "Yeah, we can do that, too."

Quick as a flash, Sideswipe, Strongarm and Bumblebee shifted into vehicle mode and zoomed out of the scrapyard.

Speeding through the forest, the Autobots traced Russell and Denny's trail back to the old arcade. Their radar screens blipped faster and louder, indicating that the Decepticon was near.

Bumblebee and Strongarm fell back and disappeared behind a thicket of trees. There they lay in wait, and Sideswipe put his part of the plan into action.

In the distance, the red sports car saw a dark shape in the sky circling Doug's Den. At that moment, the back door opened and Doug himself exited the building, carrying a load of rubbish, which he emptied into a big metal bin. Then he went back into the arcade.

Once the coast was clear, Scuzzard dived straight down and landed on the bin, scattering rubbish everywhere. He folded his massive wings behind him and proceeded to take giant bites out of the metal with his beak.

Sideswipe watched as the Decepticon devoured the bin. With each chomp, a light shimmered over his body, and Scuzzard grew larger in size. He squawked with evil glee and continued his metal meal.

From across the street, Sideswipe got ready. Then he drove into the empty parking lot of the arcade.

He revved his engine.

VROOOM! VROOOM!

Scuzzard was so engrossed in his food,

he didn't notice the vehicle behind him.

Exasperated, Sideswipe honked his horn impatiently, startling the escaped convict.

BEEEEEEEEEP!

Scuzzard choked and coughed up bits of chewed metal.

"ACK!" he gasped. "Can't a bot eat in peace? I haven't had a decent meal in five cycles!"

Sideswipe honked again.

BEEEEEEEEEP!

Scuzzard whirled around and spotted the fire-engine-red sports car made of delicious metal. "Well, well," he said, cocking his head. "Now, *that* looks like a decent meal!" Scuzzard stretched his wings and leaped toward Sideswipe.

The Autobot reversed, kicking up gravel, and pulled a 180-degree turn. Then he burned rubber right out of the car park.

"Team Bee," the hero called into his radio. "The birdbot has flown the coop ... and he's coming right at me!"

"Perfect," Bumblebee responded. "Now lead him to us!"

Scuzzard watched as his savoury snack raced away.

"I love it when they play hard to eat," he said to himself.

The Decepticon soared high into the air for an aerial view of Sideswipe. Once the Autobot was in his sights, Scuzzard swept down to attack.

"It's dinnertime!" he shouted in delight.

CHAPTER SIX

SIDESWIPE SENSED HIS ATTACKER gaining on him, and he barrelled off the main road and into the nearby forest.

The Decepticon peered through the treetops. Every couple of seconds, Sideswipe's red body became visible among the lush green foliage.

"These peculiar organic objects may provide you temporary cover, my tender morsel, but your brightness betrays you," Scuzzard said. "You're as good as digested!"

Scuzzard dived into the trees, ripping through the thick branches easily.

Sideswipe was inches away from the razor-sharp talons of his airborne adversary. He slammed on the brakes and came to a screeching halt. Scuzzard passed right over him, grazing the Autobot with his claws.

"Hey, watch the paint job, metal mouth!" Sideswipe shouted.

Scuzzard was slightly taken aback by the talking vehicle.

"Hmm, looks like my next meal is more than meets the eye," he said, squinting.

Sideswipe drove into a clearing and switched into his bot mode.

"If there's even the tiniest scratch on me, you'll be eating liquid fuel for a cycle!" he shouted.

"It appears that there is an Autobot among us," the Decepticon hissed.

He landed and folded his wings. Then he extended to his full height, towering over Sideswipe.

The young hero hadn't realised how big the Decepticon was. From afar, he had seemed like an easy enough challenge.

"Mamabot told me not to play with my food, but tearing *you* apart is going to be fun!" Scuzzard gloated.

He slowly advanced towards Sideswipe. The hot-headed Autobot started to lose his cool. He whispered into his communicator.

"Hey, guys? I could really use some back-up right about now."

"We're trying to find you," Bumblebee responded.

"If you had stayed on course and met us at the rendezvous point, this wouldn't be an issue," Strongarm added.

Sideswipe quickly glanced around. Strongarm was right. He was in the wrong part of the woods. He must have lost his way when he was trying to outrun the Decepticon.

Scuzzard sharpened his bladed fingertips against one another. The metal sparked and shrieked, causing Sideswipe to wince.

"This will not be quick, Autobot," rasped the criminal.

"But quick is what I do best," Sideswipe replied, and turned to race away out of the clearing.

But, just as quickly, Scuzzard pounced.

He hit the Autobot square in the back, pinning him to the ground. Sinking into the dirt, Sideswipe struggled under the massive weight of the Decepticon.

"You're barely a snack!" Scuzzard said.

"You don't want to eat me," grunted Sideswipe. "I'll just get stuck in your intake valve."

"On the contrary," replied Scuzzard. "Since my incarceration, I've built up quite an appetite."

"Then eat this!" Sideswipe yelled. He grabbed a fistful of mud and hurled it at Scuzzard's face.

The Decepticon reeled back.

Sideswipe rolled onto his feet.

"Yuck! What *was* that?" spat Scuzzard.

Sideswipe thought quickly. "It's a very

toxic and poisonous Earth element. It will instantly deactivate you!"

Scuzzard fell to his knees and choked. "Curse you, Autobot!" he gasped.

Sideswipe couldn't believe his luck. *The bigger they are, the dumber they are,* he thought.

Quickly shifting into his vehicle form, Sideswipe drove further into the forest to look for his friends.

A yellow blur rushed right past him and Sideswipe swerved to follow. "Bumblebee!" he cried.

The team leader reversed and pulled up next to the sports car.

Strongarm, in her police-car form, rolled up seconds later.

"What's the status report?" she asked.

"And where is the Decepticon?" added Bumblebee.

As Sideswipe prepared to tell his tale, a dark shadow swooped by overhead.

SCREEECH!

"Heads up!" Strongarm warned.

The vulture-like Decepticon descended on the red sports car, landing on Sideswipe's roof.

"Nice try, slick," Scuzzard said, folding his wings. "You had me going for a nanocycle, but I'm still active. Only now, I'm angry!"

He raked his sharp talons across the young hero, making Sideswipe yelp.

Bumblebee and Strongarm surrounded Sideswipe and Scuzzard.

"Let me guess," the villain sneered.

"More Autobots in disguise?"

"You got that right, criminal!" Strongarm shouted. She shifted into her bot mode, and so did Bumblebee.

"You are under arrest by order of the Cybertronian Police Force!" he said.

"Ha!" rasped Scuzzard. "Don't make me laugh, law-bot. We're not on Cybertron any more!"

Scuzzard lunged at the heroes, extending his bladed wings. Bumblebee and Strongarm backflipped out of the criminal's razor-sharp reach. The Decepticon landed with a thud.

With his body and his pride wounded, Sideswipe raced away. He drove behind a row of trees and changed back into his bot mode.

Bumblebee and Strongarm were ready for battle. They produced their plasma cannons and aimed them at the Decepticon.

"Fire!" Bumblebee commanded.

CHOOM! CHOOM!

The laser beams whizzed past the vulture. He evaded the blasts by soaring into the air.

"I'm just as equipped as you are," says Scuzzard, as he fired a series of bladed missiles from his wings.

FWIP! FWIP! FWIP!

"Aerial assault!" Strongarm cried.

The knife-like projectiles sliced through the air, stabbing everything in their path.

Bumblebee and Strongarm raced for cover, but as they ran, one of the bladed

darts nicked Bumblebee on the leg – and
he stumbled and fell.

"ARGH!"

Strongarm aimed her blaster from
behind a tree and fired at the birdbot.

ZAP!

The energy burst caught Scuzzard.

"Direct hit!" she cheered.

But as Scuzzard fell back, he unleashed another volley of missiles. The last dart hit Strongarm. She span around, reeling from the hit.

Scuzzard reconfigured himself into his large, intimidating bot form and sauntered over.

He picked Strongarm up in a tight grip and held her high above the ground. Wincing with pain, she kicked at her assailant, but she couldn't escape.

Still holding Strongarm, Scuzzard walked over to the limping leader and prepared to pound him into the ground with his gigantic foot.

"Lucky me," hissed Scuzzard. "I've found an all-you-can-eat Autobot buffet!"

CHAPTER SEVEN

FROM HIS HIDING PLACE, SIDESWIPE mustered up his courage and rushed to the rescue, pulling Bumblebee away from imminent bashing in the nick of time!

The young Autobot helped the wounded leader to lean against a thick tree trunk. "I'm sorry!" he cried. "This is all my fault. I should have stuck to the plan!"

"We can't worry about that now," grunted Bumblebee. "I need you to focus on a new plan!"

Bumblebee aimed the plasma cannon at his wounded leg. He set the blaster to emit an extremely fine laser beam and mended the gash in his plating.

"Whoa," Sideswipe exclaimed. "You are a real tough-bot, Bee!"

The young Autobot was thoroughly impressed with his leader. *Maybe Strongarm is right to look up to him,* he thought. *Oh, no! Strongarm!*

Sideswipe peeked out from behind a tree to see his team-mate still struggling in Scuzzard's clutches.

"Time to put my moves to good use again," Sideswipe said.

He jumped onto the nearest tree branch with ninja-like stealth and speed. Then he jumped from one to the next until he had completely disappeared into the leaves above.

Ignoring his pain, Bumblebee spoke into his communicator.

"Strongarm, what is your status?"

"Oh, I'm just hanging around!" she said, gruffly.

"If Strongarm is making jokes, we must really be in trouble!" Sideswipe quipped.

"Focus, everybot. Sideswipe will be dropping in unexpectedly. Strongarm, disengage!"

"Yes, sir!"

Strongarm shifted into vehicle mode, causing Scuzzard to loosen his grip. Then she opened her boot, catching him on the beak with the full force of an uppercut punch.

BAM!

Scuzzard's head snapped back, and he dropped the police car.

The deranged Decepticon changed into

his bird form and flew up into the air.
Before he could escape, Sideswipe
propelled himself from the treetops and
landed on top of Scuzzard.

They spiralled back onto the ground,
and the Autobot drilled Scuzzard
beakfirst into the dirt.

Before the Decepticon could recover,
Sideswipe shifted into his vehicle form
and drove into Scuzzard, hitting the
Decepticon with his bumper and
smashing him hard against a tree.

Scuzzard dropped to the ground,
wheezing and coughing.

Sideswipe was mad at Scuzzard for
hurting his friends, as well as being cross
at himself for putting them in danger.
He revved his engine and prepared to

strike again. His tyres raced, splattering dirt into the air.

"Enough!" Bumblebee shouted sternly at the red sports car. "Throttle back, Sideswipe. The battle is over."

Sideswipe pulled back and shifted into his bot mode. He stood aside so that Bumblebee and Strongarm, now in bot form, could use their neo-forges.

Combining their forces, the heroes trapped the Scavengebot in a glowing net of paralysing energy.

"You mess with Team Bee, you're gonna get stung!" Sideswipe growled.

Scuzzard thrashed against his bonds. "Look at the brave little Autobot now. But you don't fool me. I've seen how scared you really are."

Sideswipe took a step back as
Bumblebee and Strongarm tightened
their grip on the villain.

"Before this day is done, I am going to
feast on all of you!" Scuzzard sneered.

"Ugh, creepy!" Strongarm said, with
a shudder.

Scuzzard snapped his beak at her. "Permission to treat the perpetrator as hostile, Lieutenant?" Strongarm asked Bumblebee.

Before her commanding officer could answer, Strongarm judo-chopped the vulture, knocking him out.

KAPOW!

"Wow," Sideswipe said, coming to a slow realisation. "Strong. Arm. Now I get it!"

Strongarm let out an unexpected laugh and quickly regained her composure.

Bumblebee put his arms around his team-mates. "If you want respect, you have to be the first to give it," he said. "How else will we succeed as a team?"

Sideswipe and Strongarm exchanged

glances. Their leader was right.

"Let's get back to the command centre," Bumblebee said.

Back at the scrapyard, Russell and Denny were repairing the pinball machine inside Denny's garage.

Fixit rolled in and said, "I am very interested in seeing your workstop … chop … shop!"

"Come in!" Denny said, with a big smile. He motioned his arm in a grand sweeping gesture. "Welcome to my sanctuary!"

Fixit turned in a complete circle, taking in his new surroundings. There were several benches and shelves completely covered with numerous pieces of hardware, and all kinds of items in various stages of repair.

"It just looks like more of the scrapyard," Fixit said.

"That's what I keep telling him," Russell replied.

As Denny tinkered with his tools, he wiped the sweat off his brow.

Fixit focused his ocular sensors onto Denny's forehead.

"It appears you are losing fluids, Denny Clay," he said. "Perhaps one of your pipe valves has sprung a leak?"

Before Denny could reply, Grimlock squeezed his massive frame into the garage.

"We just got word from Bumblebee,"

the dinobot announced. "They captured the Decepticon! Woo-hoo!"

Grimlock started dancing, and the rumbling vibrations rattled the delicate pinball machine. The legs started to wobble and pop off one by one.

"I think there may be one too many dinobots in my garage," Denny whispered to Russell.

"What am I supposed to do with him?" Russell asked. "It's not like I can take him for a walk or a run at the dog park."

"Exercise is a wonderful idea," Denny said, tousling Russell's hair. "Why don't you practise some rugby? I'm sure Gridlock Grimlock is up for it."

"Great idea!" Russell grinned at his father, who had already started tinkering with the pinball machine again.

"Did someone call upon the lob-ball legend?" Fixit asked.

The dinobot perked up. He reconfigured himself into bot mode and cried, "GAME ON!"

Grimlock picked up Fixit in the palm of his hand.

"Release me at once," Fixit demanded.

"No, Grimlock," Denny responded, with a smile. "I meant you and Rusty could throw around the old pigskin."

"Pigskin!" said Grimlock. "Is that another Decepticon? Let me at 'im!"

"Yes," begged Fixit. "Throw him around for a change!"

"No, no, no," Russell said, shaking his head. "Pigskin is another term for a ball!"

Grimlock placed Fixit back on the ground and bounded out of the workshop, yelling, "The legend has returned!"

Denny hugged the pinball machine close and breathed a sigh of relief.

Minutes later, Russell and Grimlock were in the scrapyard taking turns to throw a rugby ball to each other.

Russell reared back and released the ball, spiralling it through the air at immense speed. Grimlock sprinted after it, pushing his massive robot form to its limit, and dived to catch it. He snatched the ball out of the air.

Unfortunately, Grimlock's movement made him an unstoppable force. He landed hard and skidded uncontrollably –

right into the command centre!

SMASH!

Russell watched helplessly as the events seem to unfold in slow motion.

Grimlock bashed straight into one of the stasis pods, cracking the surface.

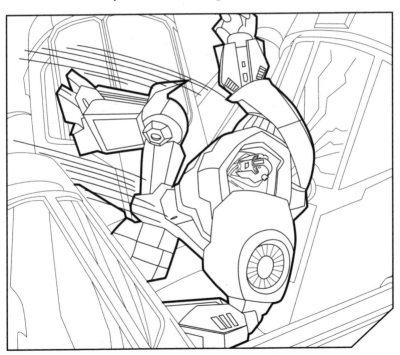

The chamber tipped over and broke.

A loud hissing sound came from within, and a sharp metallic claw scraped away at the debris. Russell ran as fast as he could to his dad's workshop.

"Dad! Fixit!" he yelled. "HELP!"

Grimlock groaned as he got back to his feet. He turned around to see the shimmering black figure of a Decepticon he recognised – an evil Corvicon called Filch!

The Corvicon slunk out of the chamber and stretched her robot limbs while emitting a high-pitched shriek.

"I'M FREE!"

Then she flapped her wings and took off into the air.

Grimlock watched the prisoner escape.

"Oh, scrap!" he whispered. They'd caught one Decepticon – but now there was another one on the loose!

CHAPTER EIGHT

THE TREK BACK TO THE COMMAND centre through the forest was long and winding. The Autobots had created this path so they could travel unobserved by humans.

Bumblebee, Sideswipe and Strongarm took turns carrying Scuzzard's unconscious form. Everybot was lost in thought.

Bumblebee contemplated how the members of his crew needed more field training and how they couldn't rely on luck to accomplish their missions, like they had today.

As if reading Bumblebee's mind, Sideswipe broke the silence.

"I want to apologise again about what happened back there," the young Autobot said. "I messed things up."

"It's all right, Sideswipe," Bumblebee said. "Any one of us could have got lost on this unfamiliar terrain."

"Not only that," Sideswipe said. "I'm mad at myself for being scared and running off. That's not like me. I'm tougher than that. Stronger than that!"

"Toughness is not a sign of strength," Strongarm said.

"Strongarm is right," Bumblebee added. "You're very good at what you do, and we are all still learning how to work as a team."

Suddenly, a message crackled in through his audio receptors. Bumblebee could barely make out what it was, but he knew it was coming from the command centre.

"ZZZK-help-ZZZZK-trouble!"

"Listen up, everybot!" Bumblebee said. "There seems to be a problem. Let's hurry up and return to base."

As the Autobots charged forward, a dark figure swooped overhead. It screeched loudly as it dive-bombed towards Team Bee.

The Autobots covered their audio receptors, losing their grip on the tied-up troublemaker, Scuzzard.

"SHINY!" Filch squawked, eyeing the metallic sheen of Scuzzard's body.

She dug her talons into his back, and the sharp pain jostled him awake.

"AAAH!" Scuzzard cried.

Filch quickly extended her wings with expert grace and speed, lifting Scuzzard into the air. The Autobots watched in dismay as she carried him away.

Scuzzard hurled insults at his attacker

until both fugitives were far beyond the reach of the Autobots.

Sideswipe blinked in disbelief and turned to Strongarm.

"Sweet Solus Prime!" he exclaimed. "Was that—"

"Yes," Strongarm replied.

"Did she just—"

"Yes."

"Are we in deep—"

"Oh, yes."

Bumblebee managed to complete their sentences. "Did a new Decepticon just fly off with the one we'd captured?"

"YES!" Strongarm and Sideswipe yelled together.

"Scrud!" Bumblebee exclaimed.

The Autobots immediately shifted from

their robot forms into their vehicle modes. They raced at top speed towards the command centre.

"Something must have happened at our base," Strongarm said, anxiously. "How else could Filch have escaped her stasis pod?"

"The sooner we get to the bottom of this, the sooner we can settle the score with those Decepticons," Sideswipe addded. He revved his engine and raced past Bumblebee and Strongarm, kicking up a cloud of exhaust and dust.

Bumblebee watched Sideswipe disappear down the hill before them. "OK, Strongarm, we have to stay calm. What do you remember about Filch?"

"Filch is a Corvicon," Strongarm

stated. "She has a compulsion to hoard objects with extremely shiny and reflective surfaces. That explains her seizure of Scuzzard."

"We need to keep our optic sensors wide and be ready for anything," Bumblebee replied.

Finally, the Autobots arrived at the scrapyard and changed back into bot mode. Sideswipe was already assessing all the devastation inside the command centre.

The outer wall had been reduced to a pile of rubble when Grimlock ploughed through it. A cloud of plaster dust still hung in the air.

Fortunately, most of the computers and monitors were still up and running,

but the communication devices were
all broken.

Grimlock, Fixit, Russell and Denny
were huddled around the stasis pods. The
chamber that had held Filch was lying on
its side, open and littered with debris.

"I'm such a klutz-o-tron!" Grimlock
cried miserably.

"What happened?" Bumblebee asked.

Russell recounted the events that had
led to Filch's escape.

Bumblebee consoled the dinobot.

"It's all right, Grimlock. Let's look at
the fuel gauge as half full, shall we?
Come on, team!"

He hoped that his positive attitude
would be contagious.

"But how can I?" Grimlock wailed.

"This was a massive mistake!"

Denny stepped in and tried to lighten the mood. "It just so happens that Fixit has been itching to repair something all day. Maybe this is an opportunity in disguise?"

"Great to hear," Bumblebee said.

"Well, little buddies," Denny said to Fixit and Russell, "the old pinball machine can wait."

With his dad, Russell grabbed the end of the stasis pod and they lifted it upright. Fixit reconfigured his arm into a hyper-span regulator so that he could begin repairs on the damaged chamber.

Strongarm turned to her team leader and asked, "What's our next course of action, sir?"

Bumblebee crossed over to the command centre's main console and pulled up the holo-scroll. "It appears there are two active Decepticon signals in our vicinity. It must be Scuzzard and Filch."

"They haven't got far," Sideswipe said. "If we act fast, we could still catch up with them!"

"We'll *have* to act fast," Strongarm added. "Or else they'll fly into the city and put all those civilians at risk."

"Precisely, Strongarm," Bumblebee said. "This time we'll need to combine all our forces to take them down. Are you ready?"

Grimlock lifted his head with pride as the team leader looked his way.

"Here's what we're going to do, Team Bee," Bumblebee commanded. "Get out there and cage those birdbots!"

CHAPTER NINE

THE SUN WAS SETTING OVER Crown City, and its citizens were unaware of two large winged creatures soaring together high above the skyline.

Filch was flying towards the amusement park, attracted by its blinking lights and bright, colourful surfaces. She planned to build a new nest on top of the Ferris wheel.

"SHINY!" she squealed.

Scuzzard was less enthusiastic.

"Unhand me at once!" he commanded.

Filch ignored her captive.

Furious, Scuzzard bit down hard on the Corvicon's foot.

Filch howled in pain and dropped the

Scavengebot down, right into an empty bumper car ride.

SMASH!

Looking around, Scuzzard was pleased with his new surroundings.

"This isn't exactly the central plaza at Kaon, but it definitely deserves a good thrashing," Scuzzard said. "It's hideous!"

He immediately laid waste to the bumper cars. Once they were reduced to scrap, he ate them one by one. As he swallowed each one, his body shimmered and increased in size. Soon he was as big as the ride itself!

The Decepticon burst through the roof. He loomed ominously over the amusement park, casting a dark shadow with his imposing form.

"I'm large and in charge!" Scuzzard cackled.

The Scavengebot set his sights on the scrumptious skyline of Crown City in the distance.

"Now, there's the main course!"

Fearing that her new territory was being threatened, Filch dive-bombed toward Scuzzard. She head-butted him in the chest, knocking him off balance.

BAM!

The gigantic robot jumped up and raced through the arcade and out towards Crown City. He'd just made it to the car park of Doug's Den when Filch caught up to him and torpedoed towards him once again. The massive monster plucked his flying foe out of the air and crunched her in his grip.

"You won't catch me off-guard this time, but I'll catch you!" he jeered.

At that very moment, Bumblebee and his team of Autobots sped into the car park. Grimlock looked up in awe.

"Whoa! Scavengebot versus Corvicon? This is a better battle than in the Rumbledome back home!" he shouted.

Scuzzard turned his attention toward the new arrivals and smiled wickedly. "The fun has just begun! Let's play whack-a-bot!"

He stomped and pounded the pavement with his enormous feet as the heroes scrambled to evade being crushed. They dodged the assault from above, narrowly missing one another.

"Ha! Now I'll get to see some Autobot bumper cars in action!" Scuzzard said, with a laugh.

"Your wish is our command sequence!" Sideswipe cried, burning rubber.

With that, he slammed right into the Decepticon's foot.

BAM!

"Way to take the lead, Sideswipe," Bumblebee said.

Bumblebee and Strongarm followed their friend and bashed into the humongous Decepticon's other foot.

They drove in reverse and then slammed into his feet again, as if they really were bumper cars!

"Enough games," Scuzzard bellowed. "You are nothing but nanodrones to me!"

He hurled Filch at the Autobots, and she landed on top of Bumblebee. The yellow sports car and the Corvicon sped across the car park until they came to a screeching halt.

Strongarm raced over to her lieutenant's side.

"Keep that Scavengebot occupied until we can regroup!" she called out to Sideswipe and Grimlock.

"Hey, birdbrain!" Grimlock shouted at Scuzzard. "I've taken down bigger bots than you with my Dino-Destructo Double Drop!"

"I'd be shocked if that were true," Scuzzard replied, with a sneer. "But I'm willing to let you try. Dinobots make me laugh!"

The Decepticon advanced on Grimlock and knelt down to face him.

Sideswipe used the opportunity to change into his bot mode and spring into action. He sprinted towards a nearby lamppost, swung around it with the agility of an acrobat, and leapt onto an adjacent telephone pole. Then he hurled himself off the top and landed right on Scuzzard's back.

"Let's get ready to Rumbledome!" Sideswipe yelled.

The flashy Autobot punched the Decepticon right in the head.

POW!

Grimlock followed suit and jumped onto Scuzzard, too.

SMASH!

"You've got double trouble now!" he quipped, and bashed the big robot with his tail.

In the meantime, Strongarm changed into her robot form as she reached Bumblebee. She pushed Filch off the team leader. The Decepticon twitched and started to stir.

Bumblebee revived first and quickly shifted into bot mode.

"We have to stop Scuzzard!" he exclaimed.

Strongarm guided his gaze to the gargantuan villain. "He's got a lot on his mind right now, sir," he said.

Bumblebee beamed with pride watching his team finally work together.

Suddenly, a screeching voice pierced

their audio receptors.

"SHINY!"

Filch was back on her feet and ready to attack.

Bumblebee and Strongarm deployed their neo-forges again, willing them to take the shape of an energy staff and a crossbow.

Filch charged Bumblebee, pecking at him with her beak. The Autobot parried with the staff and directed an energy blast at his flying foe.

ZAP!

The Decepticon fell to the ground.

Strongarm shot an energised grappling hook from her crossbow that looped all around Filch's body. The Corvicon hissed and bucked as the glowing rope tied tight.

"We got us a live one here, sir!" Strongarm grunted.

On the other side of the arcade's car park, Sideswipe and Grimlock continued to attack Scuzzard together.

Grimlock threw a jab.

WHACK!

Sideswipe followed with a right hook.

WHAP!

Grimlock landed an uppercut.

WHAM!

Disoriented, the Decepticon flailed his arms. One of them caught Grimlock and swatted the dinobot onto the ground.

THUD!

Scuzzard lifted his leg and prepared to make street pizza out of Grimlock.

Sideswipe acted fast and covered the Scavengebot's optic sensors with his hands. Scuzzard whirled around blindly while the Autobot guided him towards a telephone pole.

Scuzzard stumbled and his upper body got tangled in the power lines. Sideswipe swiftly slid down the pole to safety as volts of electricity surged through the wires and overloaded the Decepticon in a shower of sparks!

ZaaaaaaaaRK!

Scuzzard spasmed and jolted as he shrank back to his normal size. Finally, he slumped headfirst into a crumpled, smouldering heap.

Boom!

"Aw, yeah!" Sideswipe cheered. "Team Bee always brings the buzz!"

Grimlock laughed. "Yeah, he looks a little *shocked*!"

All of a sudden, more electricity crackled behind the duo. They turned to see an illuminated portal light up the night sky.

It was a Groundbridge, one of the

ways the Autobots travelled to other worlds.

"What now?" growled Grimlock.

But from it emerged their team-mate Drift. "I believe I can be of some assistance," he said.

"Nah, we got everything under control," replied Sideswipe.

Suddenly, someone screamed.

"AAAAAAAAH!"

Sideswipe, Grimlock, and Drift turned to see Strongarm hoisted off the ground. She was clutching her crossbow, which was attached to Filch, who was soaring high into the air!

The Corvicon flapped her wings faster and faster, dragging the Autobot along for a wild ride.

Pulling Scuzzard behind them, the other three Autobots all rushed back over to their leader.

"What's the plan, Bee?" Sideswipe cried as he ran.

"Gridlock Grimlock!" Bumblebee exclaimed, using the dinobot's lob-ball legend name.

"Reporting for duty," the dinobot called out.

"I need your lob-ball skills," Bumblebee said. "Can you throw?"

"Throw what?" Grimlock asked.

"Me!" Bumblebee yelled.

As the dinobot realised Bumblebee's plan, he picked up their leader and threw him high into the air. Bumblebee flew through the night sky like a rocket and

reached Strongarm in seconds.

Bumblebee gripped on to Strongarm's
feet, and their combined weight slowed
Filch down. Filch flapped as hard as she
could, but the Autobots were too heavy.
She flew down low, towards the ground.

At that very moment, Doug came out of the arcade to investigate the commotion behind his store – and was immediately dumbstruck!

He saw Drift and Sideswipe standing over Scuzzard, and Grimlock watching Bumblebee and Strongarm crash to the ground with Filch.

"Scrap!" Sideswipe shouted when he saw the man. "Let's make tracks!"

Sideswipe and the bounty hunter, Drift, dragged Scuzzard into the Groundbridge, that was still shining brightly in the sky like a star.

Grimlock helped Bumblebee and Strongarm yank Filch into the portal before it closed behind them. There was a flash, and the robots disappeared.

Doug took off his glasses, rubbed his eyes, and puts the glasses back on.

"I must be playing too many video games," he said.

CHAPTER TEN

TEAM BEE ZIPPED OVER THE groundbridge and appeared at the scrapyard in an instant. The Autobots found themselves behind the tall tower of cars where Grimlock had been napping earlier that morning.

Fixit contacted them from the command centre.

"Is everybot in one piece?" he asked.

Before they could answer, Filch saw the cars and screeched.

"MORE SHINY!" she squawked.

In a flash, she expanded her powerful wings, shoving Bumblebee and Strongarm to the ground. The other Autobots gave chase, but the Corvicon was too fast.

Filch flew up to the top of the tower and heaved it with all her might. Tipping and toppling, the cars came crashing down in an avalanche of heavy metal.

"Brace yourselves!" Drift shouted.

With lightning speed, the bounty hunter unsheathed his energy sword and cleaved the first falling car in half. Then he nimbly somersaulted backwards, out of harm's way.

Bumblebee and the others fired their blasters at the vehicles, but the toppling metal was too much.

CHOOM!

CHOOM!

SLAM!

Drift watched in horror as his teammates were buried under a pile of cars.

Then he saw Filch heading towards the command centre. He was faced with a decision: save his team-mates or stop the Decepticon?

Bumblebee emitted a muffled cry.

"Drift ... help ... "

"Jetstorm, Slipstream," Drift called out. "Heed your master!"

Jetstorm and Slipstream were Drift's mini-con apprentices who lived in his armour. At his command, they hopped off his armour and sprang into action.

"The captive Corvicon has escaped ... again!" announced Drift. "But I must assist my fellow soldiers."

"Of course, master. We're off!"

Jetstorm and Slipstream bowed and then zipped after Filch. Fixit uploaded coordinates directly into their mainframes, instructing them where to guide the Corvicon.

As the mini-cons zigzagged through the scrapyard, they scraped their limbs across the metal nearby. The screeching sound and shower of sparks caught Filch's attention.

She honed in on the mini-cons and squealed.

"So SHINY! For my collection!"

Jetstorm and Slipstream banked left. Filch dived after them and chased the mini-cons until they came to a clearing in the scrapyard.

And at the end of the clearing, Denny, Russell, and Fixit were waiting for them — driving the hydraulic truck!

The two mini-cons split up and zoomed in opposite directions, confusing the speeding Corvicon. She flapped her wings to slow down, but it was too late.

Denny activated the magnet and pulled Filch straight out of the sky!

CLANG!

The Decepticon dangled helplessly, screeching in distress.

"Looks like we're adding you back into *our* collection," Russell replied.

The Autobots reconvened at the command centre. They looked a little worse for wear but were relieved that the Decepticon disaster was finally brought to an end.

Together, they deposited Scuzzard and Filch back into their repaired stasis pods.

"Who says there's never any excitement at the scrapyard?" Sideswipe said, with a smile.

Russell smiled back. "To be honest, I wouldn't mind some quiet time."

"We can always play pinball!" Denny added with a laugh.

As the group laughed, Bumblebee turned to Drift and said, "Thank you for your assistance today."

"Think nothing of it," Drift said. "I am part of the team."

"Agreed," Bumblebee nodded. He looked at Strongarm, Sideswipe, Fixit, and Grimlock. "There is no problem too big that can't be handled with teamwork," he said.

"And that includes a three-story tall Decepticon!" Sideswipe added.

"We accomplished our mission and became better team-mates thanks to you, sir," Strongarm said to Bumblebee. "Optimus Prime would be very proud."

"Speaking of phenomenal forces," Drift interrupted. "There is indeed a batch of Energon in a quadrant not too far from here. We can set our course for the power source in the morning."

"Awesome," Bumblebee said. "It will definitely give us an advantage in future battles against the Decepticons."

"I agree with you, boss," Grimlock told his leader. "But don't you think we all deserve to recharge a bit? I know I do."

And with that, the dinobot curled up outside the command centre and fell fast asleep.

··· MISSION COMPLETE ···

CALLING ALL AUTOBOTS

We have a Transformers toy bundle to giveaway!

If you want to be in with a chance to receive this awesome prize just answer this question:

WHO IS THE LEADER OF TEAM BEE?

Write your answer on the back of a postcard and send it to:
Transformers Competition
Hachette Children's Group
Carmelite House, 50 Victoria Embankment
London, EC4Y 0DZ

Closing Date: September 30th 2016
For full terms and conditions go to www.hachettechildrens.co.uk/terms

THE ALL-NEW ACTION-PACKED ADVENTURES

OUT NOW ON DVD & DIGITAL HD

© 2016 Hasbro, all rights reserved.

PRIMAL [SCREEN]   Hasbro STUDIOS